WILLIAM
HENRY HARRISON
YOUNG TIPPECANOE

Written by
Howard Peckham

Illustrated by
Cathy Morrison

J B
HARRISON

Patria Press, Inc.
3842 Wolf Creek Circle
Carmel, IN 46033
Phone 877-736-7930

Printed and bound in the United States of America

10 9 8 7 6 5 4 3 2 1

Text originally published by the Bobbs-Merrill Co., 1951 in the
Childhood of Famous Americans Series.® The Childhood of
Famous Americans Series® is a registered trademark of
Simon & Schuster, Inc.

Library of Congress Cataloging-in-Publication Data

Peckham, Howard Henry, 1910–1995
    William Henry Harrison, young Tippecanoe / written by
Howard Peckham; illustrated by Cathy Morrison.
    p. cm.
    SUMMARY: A biography focusing on the early years of the man
who distinguished himself at the Battle of Tippecanoe and was later
elected the ninth president of the United States.
    ISBN: 1-882859-03-0
    1. Harrison, William Henry, 1773–1841—Childhood and youth
Juvenile literature. 2. Presidents—United States—Biography
Juvenile literature. [1. Harrison, William Henry, 1773–1841
Childhood and youth. 2. Presidents.] I. Morrison, Cathy, ill. II. Title.

E392 .P33 1999
973.5'8'092--dc21
[B]   99-047881

Edited by: Harold Underdown
Designed by: inari

Contents

Illustrations

Chapter 1

The Ducking

Three boys and a girl came galloping down the slope to the river. Each one was whipping the flank of an imaginary horse. They rode furiously into the shipyard. The boy in the lead waved a wooden sword with his other hand.

"They're heading for the river, Captain!" he called.

"After them, Colonel!" his sister answered.

Billy Harrison was playing his favorite game. He was Colonel "Light-Horse" Harry Lee, Virginia's famous cavalry leader of the American Revolution. Like Lee, he was attacking the British. His "troop" was made up of his sister Sally, aged ten, Ezra and Josh, children of the Harrison family's slaves, and Smoky, the family's spaniel.

The children nearly always played war games. The war had been going on ever since Billy could remember. Now, in the summer of 1780, he was seven years old, and the colonies still seemed far away from victory.

Billy led his troop across the shipyard and onto the dock in the James River. They jumped into the old barge tied there. They all stopped then, panting from the run.

"Too late," Billy said. "There they go — the cowards!"

Even Smoky stared across the broad, peaceful river. Nothing was moving. He barked once, anyway, as if he understood the game.

"Oh, Billy, I'm tired!" Sally dropped down on a seat in the barge.

Billy looked at her. She wasn't his loyal captain any longer. She was just a flushed fair-haired girl. His cavalrymen were only two boys dangling their bare feet in the water. His sword was just a stick after all. The pursuit, which had been so vivid to Billy, faded away. He sighed and folded up his slight frame in the bow of the boat.

"What shall we do now?" Billy asked.

"Can't we sit for a minute? You're so restless today, Billy!"

"What I'd like to do is go and join the militia, like Carter."

"Master Carter looked mighty fine in his uniform when he rode off yesterday," Ezra put in.

"And Benjy's been away so long I can't even remember how he looks. I *wish* I hadn't been the youngest boy."

Sally knew what he meant. "Berkeley isn't the same," she said, "with the boys gone and Father always up in Richmond in the House of Delegates. It seems so lonely here now. I hate the war."

"So do I," said Billy. He knew there were many exciting things beyond Berkeley — things he couldn't see while the war was going on.

Just then Smoky trotted up and barked.

"Look! He wants to play. Come on, Smoky!" Billy jumped up and found a stick.

He threw it into the water. The frisky dog hesitated a moment on the edge of the boat. Then he plunged in. He swam out to the stick, caught it in his mouth, and brought it back to the barge. This was an old game and Smoky needed no coaching.

"Let me throw one," Sally begged.

Billy bent over and took the stick from Smoky's mouth. Sally waved another in front of the dog and tossed it out. At once Smoky turned and paddled off to retrieve it. On the dock Josh and Ezra tried to see which could throw stones farther.

The heavy barge hardly moved as Billy and Sally stood on its edge. It had no rail, and they could lean over and touch the water easily. Once

"Look! He wants to play. Come on, Smoky!"

they lifted Smoky into the boat to let him rest. He shook himself vigorously.

"O-o-o-ooh!" Sally screamed as the drops of cool water sprayed on her. She jumped to one side. Her foot came down on a stick and she lost her balance. "Billy!"

He was on his knees beside Smoky. He looked up to see his sister falling sideways into the river. *Splash!* Billy lurched to the side of the boat. Sally couldn't swim! When her head bobbed up he reached for her. Her long wet hair was plastered over her eyes and she couldn't see his hand. She went under again. Ezra and Josh came running.

This time when her head came up, Billy shouted, "Sally! Here!"

She flailed her arms wildly and came nearer. He stretched out as far as he could reach.

"Grab her, Master Billy!"

Billy was scared. What could they do? Sally started to go down again.

"That's the third time, Master Billy," cried Ezra. "Miss Sally will drown!"

As Sally's arm sank down, Billy caught it and held on tightly. For a second he thought her weight would pull him over the side. Then he felt hands seize his belt. "We'll hold you, Master Billy," Josh promised.

Billy clung to Sally's arm and pulled her nearer. With her other arm she groped for the barge. She

She flailed her arms wildly and came nearer.

was gasping for air. Billy clutched her dress and then helped her swing one leg up and over. He and Josh and Ezra all pulled together. Sally rolled into the barge.

"Are you all right?" Billy asked anxiously.

Sally lay face down, choking. Billy slapped her on the back. That did no good. Then he stepped astride his sister and bent over. With one hand on each side of her waist he lifted her. It was all he could do to raise her. Sally was much larger than he, and now she was as limp as her rag doll. With her head and feet down, Sally coughed up the water she had swallowed. Billy's arms ached but he held her until she sputtered and gasped. Then he let her down gently.

"Oh dear!" she said.

Billy was so relieved he laughed.

Sally sat up and leaned back against the side of the barge. She still looked pale and shaky.

"You all right?" Billy repeated.

She nodded. "You saved my life, Billy. I almost drowned."

"Oh, you could have climbed out." But Sally's words made Billy feel good. His heart was still pounding, but he was pleased that he had not been too scared to act when she needed his help.

Chapter 2

The Picnic

The Harrison family owned Berkeley, a plantation of several hundred acres. Besides the shipyard, Berkeley had a mill for grinding corn and wheat, a blacksmith shop, a carriage shed, and stables for cattle and horses. There were barns for drying tobacco, cribs for corn, hogpens, chicken coops and a smokehouse. Like other wealthy Virginian families, the Harrisons also owned slaves. A hundred enslaved people worked for them.

The Harrison's house stood in the center of everything, facing the James River. It was a red-brick mansion on a green lawn, with a red-brick guesthouse on one side, and a red-brick kitchen on the other. A porch shaded the back of the house where the avenue came up from the pike. Its high roof rested on three white pillars at either end.

One August morning a little procession came out the back door. First Smoky dashed out. Billy ran after him. Then came Sally, followed by Mrs. Harrison. Last of all were two house servants. The woman, Peony, carried a basket covered with a white napkin. Abe, an old man, carried a small bundle of wood and a hatchet.

When they came to the creek, both Billy and Sally ran to the mill. The building was empty and the gray-stone grinding wheels stood still. The mill ran only when the Harrisons needed corn meal or wheat flour. But the children liked to climb up on the big water wheel.

"Isn't it nice and cool up here?" Sally said. She listened to the pleasant murmur of the rapids in the creek.

Billy climbed to the very top of the wheel. He was rocking it with his weight when his mother and the servants came up. "Let's go swimming!" he called.

Sally made a face and shook her head. "I had enough water last week, thank you!"

"Why don't you just wade and find me some pretty stones to border my flower beds?" Mrs. Harrison suggested.

Billy scrambled down. He rolled up his breeches and waded into the creek. Smoky splashed in after him. Mrs. Harrison and Sally sat down on the bank, while Abe started a small fire. Peony spread a linen cloth on the grass and began to take food out of the basket. Billy waded around looking for stones. He was trying to find bits of clear quartz. Sally called it rock crystal.

"Look!" Suddenly he held up a tiny turtle. "Let's have turtle soup!"

"Oh, Billy!" Sally objected. "Don't you dare hurt that little thing! Let me have it."

Billy grinned and passed the little lump to his sister.

"Come out now, Billy," Mrs. Harrison called at last. "Here's a surprise for you."

Billy dried his feet on the grass and went over to the picnic cloth. Mrs. Harrison and Sally were already sitting by it. Peony handed him a thick triangle of bread.

Billy looked disappointed. "Aren't we going to having anything else? Didn't I smell ham frying?"

Sally giggled. "Take a bite."

Billy bit one end off his triangle. It tasted like bread and butter and ham, all at once! It was delicious. He looked at the piece of bread in amazement. Then he looked up at his mother. "Why didn't we ever have this ham-bread before?" he asked. "It's good!"

Mrs. Harrison smiled. "It's something new, Billy. Mistress Byrd heard about it the last time she was in Richmond. It's called a sandwich."

Suddenly he held up a tiny turtle. "Let's have turtle soup!"

"*Sand*wich! Is there sand in it?"

"Oh, Billy, of course not!" said Sally. "You couldn't eat it if there were."

"No, Billy, it was named after the English Earl of Sandwich," explained his mother. "The story goes that the Earl was playing cards one night with friends. The men all grew hungry and sent for some bread and meat. But when the food came they didn't like to leave their game. The Earl wanted to hold his cards with one hand, so he put his meat between two pieces of bread. The sandwich is very popular now in England, Mistress Byrd hears. And it's a good thing for a picnic."

Billy nodded. "I'll have two more — or maybe three."

After five sandwiches, fruit and cakes, Billy leaned back against the tree. He watched a cloud drift by. He felt well fed and contented. The day had turned out better than he had expected. Berkeley was a good place to be, he decided.

"How did Grandfather happen to come here?" he asked suddenly.

"His father had bought the land, and your grandfather came to live on it," his mother answered.

"I wouldn't want to live anywhere else," Sally said.

"Why, Sally, you might have been born in England if the Harrison family and my family hadn't come to this country," said Mrs. Harrison.

"I wouldn't want to be an Englishman," Billy declared.

"You're an American," Mrs. Harrison said, "but only because your ancestors came here from England."

"Why?"

"They didn't like the way they had to live there. They wanted more freedom, and believed they would find it here."

"Tell us about them," Sally urged.

"Again? All right. . . . Your father is really Benjamin Harrison the fifth."

"Just like a king?"

She laughed. "Like a king, but you know it means only that there were four earlier men in the family named Benjamin."

"Is Benjy number six?" Billy asked about his big brother.

"That's right, son. The first Benjamin lived in England, and he came over in 1632 with his wife. Virginia didn't have many people then. The oldest town was only about twenty-five years old."

"You mean Jamestown?" Sally asked.

Mrs. Harrison nodded. "This first Benjamin settled near it. He became clerk of the Virginia Council, the group of men the Governor chose to help rule the colony. Benjamin had a son — "

"Benjamin the second?"

"Yes. He was a soldier, and later a member of

the Council. He also helped start the College of William and Mary in Williamsburg."

"What about the next Benjamin?" Sally asked.

"The third one did not live to be very old. He died before his father did. But he was attorney general for Virginia and then treasurer, and he was elected to the House of Burgesses. That was what they called our legislature then. And. . . . he came up the James River and bought this land! It had belonged to Governor Berkeley and it was named for him."

"Is that how we got here?"

"Yes, dear, but not our house. The fourth Benjamin, your grandfather, built that. He was a soldier and a member of the House of Burgesses, too. But he didn't live much longer than his father had."

"Is he the one. . . " Sally began.

Mrs. Harrison nodded. "He was standing in the doorway one afternoon during a summer shower. Suddenly he was struck dead by a bolt of lightning!"

Billy sat up. He had never heard about his grandfather's death before. "Was Father with him?"

"No, that was in 1744, and Father was almost grown. He was a student at William and Mary College. He came home and took charge of the plantation."

"Did you know him then?" Sally asked.

"No, I didn't meet him till later. So you see, children, Father's family — and mine, too — have been here a long time. We have lived in Virginia and helped make it what it is. Benjy and Carter are away fighting for us today, and Father is serving as speaker of our legislature. We shouldn't complain because we can't have our family together. When our country needs help, we have to forget about ourselves and do what is needed."

"I wish I could be a soldier," said Billy.

"You're too skinny," Sally said.

"No, Billy, you have two brothers in uniform and that's enough. You must study—there will be many things to do after the war ends, and Virginia will need men who know what to do."

Billy didn't understand. After the war was over here, he was sure there wouldn't be anything exciting to do.

"What about your family, Mother?" Sally wanted to know.

"Oh, I lived at Eltham, north of here. My father died when I was young, so you never knew him. He was William Bassett the third. He was in the House of Burgesses and knew your grandfather. The second William was a colonel in the militia and a member of the Virginia Council. His father was an officer in the British army who came here about 1660. We're Virginians through and through."

Billy jumped to his feet and began marching.

"I'm a Virginian, I'm a Virginian through and through!"

Sally laughed and Mrs. Harrison got up from the ground.

"All right, young man, you can march back home now. But, first, let me tell you both one thing more. You can be proud of your ancestors, but don't forget to make your ancestors proud of you."

Billy stopped marching and looked at her. He had never thought of his family in that way before. They had done important things in Virginia and given him this fine home. Now he would show them he could do as well.

"Maybe I'll do something better," he said to himself.

Chapter 3

The Young Doctor

On a beautiful September day, several weeks later, Billy and Sally rode to the far edge of a cotton field with the overseer, Mr. Collins. Their mother was not at home. They walked their horses until Billy grew impatient. He wanted to gallop and feel the wind in his face. But the children were supposed to stay with the overseer.

Billy was on his own small horse named Brownie. He made a face at Sally and jerked the reins to show that he wanted to run. Sally nodded in understanding.

"I have to speak to the field hands here," said Mr. Collins. "If you and Master Billy will wait and rest — "

"Oh, we're not tired, Mr. Collins!"

But Mr. Collins dismounted and left them under a tree.

"I'll race you!" Billy challenged.

Sally sighed. "I hope we can go back on the road."

"I'll race you!" Billy challenged. Then he stared past her.

"What's the matter?"

"Here comes somebody — running! Looks like Ezra."

A small figure was dashing down the path toward them.

"Master Billy!" When Ezra came up he hung onto Billy's stirrup and panted. "Uncle Dave cut himself bad! He's bleedin'! Your mother's not home."

"Oh, dear!" said Sally in alarm.

"Can you help?" Ezra finished.

Mrs. Harrison always looked after any one of the family or servants who was sick or injured. Billy had often helped her. There might not be time to fetch his mother — *he* could take care of Uncle Dave.

"Sally, you ride over to Randolphs' and get Mother. I'll get the medicine basket and take it to Uncle Dave's cabin. Ezra, you tell Mr. Collins where we're going."

Billy and Sally turned their horses toward the road and trotted off in excitement. Now they had a good reason to ride fast.

Once on the road they separated. Billy urged Brownie into a gallop. She was glad to start home, and she seemed to go faster and faster. The wind whistled past Billy's ears. Brownie's pounding hoofs raised clouds of dust. Billy bent over Brownie's neck. "Come on, girl! Come on!"

She cantered to the porch and Billy pulled her up. He dropped the reins across her neck and slid off. Brownie headed at once for the stables.

Billy rushed into the house. He ran up to his mother's bedroom for her wicker medicine basket. Billy grabbed the handle and ran downstairs. The basket bumped against his legs. One of the servants had heard his clattering footsteps and met him in the lower hall.

"Uncle Dave is hurt! I'm going."

Then he was out the door and running toward the slave quarters. Several women and children stood around one cabin. They called, "Uncle Dave's in here, Master Billy!" Billy hurried in.

"You got the basket, Master Billy?" asked Josh. He sat by the pallet where his mother was tending Uncle Dave. Uncle Dave's left arm hung over the edge. Blood ran freely from a long gash above his wrist and dripped into a basin. Josh's mother was cleaning it with a cloth.

"He was sharpening a sickle when it happened," she explained.

"Sally's gone after Mother."

As he watched Billy thought something about Uncle Dave's arm looked wrong.

"Maybe his arm wouldn't bleed so much if he held it up, instead of down."

The woman raised the old man's arm.

"That helps, Master Billy. But it needs wrapping. You got any strips of clean cotton?"

Billy dug into the basket. There were strips of linen, shears, splints, salves, and bottles of herbs and medicines. Then he had an idea—he could bandage this cut himself! He had helped his mother before. Someone ought to do something for Uncle Dave right away. First, though, they would have to stop that bleeding.

"I know what Mother would do," he announced suddenly. "We need a little piece of wood or metal — a short, thin piece."

Josh jumped up and went to the table. "How about a spoon?"

"That would be fine."

Josh handed it to him. Billy took a napkin from the basket. He stretched it out by pulling on opposite corners and tied a hard knot in the center. Then he slipped it around Uncle Dave's arm. He put the knot over the artery that showed above Uncle Dave's elbow, and tied the ends of the napkin. Then he stuck the spoon in this loop and twisted it around and around. The rope of napkin grew tighter. The knot pressed against the artery and shut off the flow of blood.

"Here, Josh, you hold the spoon so it won't untwist."

Josh took hold of the spoon. Billy turned back to the basket and picked up a piece of linen. He cut off a piece and folded it to make a pad. He laid the pad over the cut, and Josh's mother held it by one corner. Then he took a long strip of cloth and wound it around and around Uncle Dave's arm. The bandage went on down to the wrist.

"It isn't very neat," Billy admitted, "but it ought to work. You can loosen the tourniquet now," he told Josh. "We have to tie this."

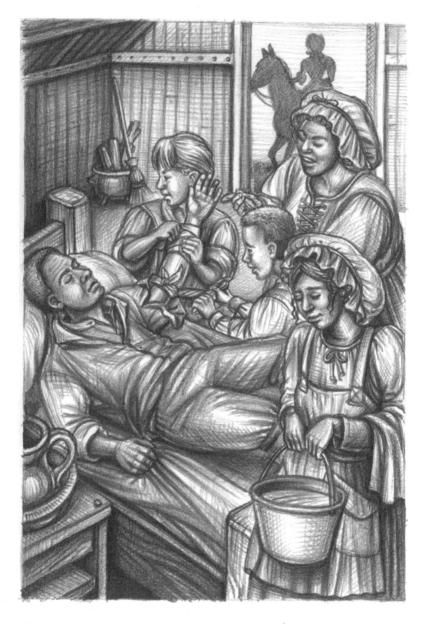

Then he took a long strip of cloth and wound it around and around Uncle Dave's arm.

It took Billy only a minute to loop the cloth around and tie a knot. "There! Does that feel better, Uncle Dave?"

"Yes sir! I thought I would bleed to death. Bless you, boy. You're a right fine doctor."

Suddenly there was a shout outside. "Here she comes! Here's Mistress Harrison!"

The group at the door fell back, and Mrs. Harrison hurried in. "What is it, David?" she began, then stopped. "Oh! Someone has taken care of you. Why, Billy, did you do this?"

Billy explained, "He was bleeding — I thought I ought to do something. So I put on a tourniquet and then we wrapped his arm — not very good. . . "

"Why, Billy, it's fine!" Mrs. Harrison said proudly. "I couldn't have done better. Does it feel all right, David?"

"Yes, ma'am. The little master, he knew what to do, just like you."

"You keep quiet today," Mrs. Harrison ordered, "and come up to the house tonight. We'll look at your arm again."

Billy felt happy. He liked to help sick people. He wondered if he should be a doctor when he grew up. It would be nice to cure people with wounds or diseases. He picked up the basket.

"Want me to carry it?" Josh offered.

Billy shook his head. The basket was a kind of badge of office. "But you can help me rub Brownie down. She was pretty hot when I jumped off."

"Sure, I'll help."

The two boys started out. Mrs. Harrison followed them. She said, "I'm very proud of you, Billy. It was important to stop that bleeding before I could get here. Your father will want to hear about this, and he — why, all of the Harrisons — will be proud of the youngest Harrison, too."

Billy grinned to himself. He was glad he had done something that would please the five Benjamins.

Chapter 4

News of a Traitor

Sally burst into the house one afternoon in late September. "Mother! Billy! Father's coming! I saw him from the garden."

Billy had been whittling a willow whistle. He dropped his knife and the wood and ran to the door. Two horsemen were riding towards the house.

"There's someone with him!"

"Father nearly always brings company from Richmond," Sally reminded him.

Mrs. Harrison followed the children out on the porch. "Why, I do believe it's Richard Henry Lee."

"Is he in the House of Delegates, too?" Sally asked.

"Yes, he is. It was Mr. Lee who first called for the Declaration of Independence."

Billy was only half listening. He wasn't interested in politics. He and Sally ran down the steps as the men dismounted.

"Well, hello, Sally, Billy!" Mr. Harrison hugged them both at once. "How are you?" he said heartily. "What have you been doing?"

Mrs. Harrison was greeting Mr. Lee. "I caught a Luna moth yesterday," Billy began at once, "and — "

"Father, I've finished my sampler," Sally interrupted.

"Fine, fine," boomed Mr. Harrison. "I want to see it."

"William Henry, you're getting taller but not much thicker," Mr. Lee said pleasantly. "The last time I visited Berkeley you were just about four. I carried you around on my shoulders one whole afternoon."

Mr. Harrison burst out laughing. "You should see him on a horse now."

Billy stared at Mr. Lee. "Are you related to Light-Horse Harry Lee, sir?"

"Yes, he's my cousin."

"Colonel Lee is a hero in this household," Mrs. Harrison explained.

"Where is he now?" Billy asked.

"Up around the Hudson River or in northern New Jersey," Mr. Lee said. "Now that Benedict Arnold is in command in that area, I believe we may expect some action."

Mr. Harrison nodded. "Arnold has planned some brilliant campaigns. Billy knows about the battle of Saratoga."

"Well, hello, Sally, Billy!" Mr. Harrison hugged them both at once.

"If he and Colonel Lee are together," Billy said, "the British had better watch out!"

Mr. Harrison said, "Sally, my lass, you lead the way in with Mr. Lee. Billy, you may take the horses to the stable and tell someone to bring in our saddlebags."

Billy scrambled up on his father's big horse and seized the reins of Mr. Lee's horse.

"What are you going to do, Ben?" Mr. Lee asked. "Make a cavalry officer of him?"

"Oh no, Richard," Mrs. Harrison said quickly. "I have two sons in uniform now. No more soldiers in the family. Billy is very good with sick people. I hope he will be a doctor."

"What do you say, William Henry?"

"I'd rather ride with your cousin." Billy touched the horse lightly with his heels and trotted off to the stables. The two men laughed. "I'm afraid you have another soldier, Mistress Harrison," said Mr. Lee.

When Billy came back to the house, it seemed much more alive. Berkeley always did when his father was at home. The house slaves hurried to set the long table for dinner. Abe carried the saddlebags upstairs. Peony was taking a tray into the drawing room. Billy could hear his father's loud, hearty voice there, and Mr. Lee's too. He hurried in.

His mother was pouring tea. Billy took a piece of cake and sat down. "Father will be home for two weeks," Sally whispered.

"How long can you stay with us?" Mrs. Harrison asked their guest.

"Only overnight. I'm on my way to Williamsburg."

Mr. Harrison looked thoughtful. "Perhaps I'll go with you, Richard. I need some papers from Williamsburg for our work on land claims.

Then you wouldn't have to ride back here. But I'm sorry to lose any time at Berkeley."

"Couldn't I go?" Billy was anxious to make a trip away from home. "I could bring the papers back for you."

"No, Billy," his mother said. "It's twenty-six miles to Williamsburg. You're too young. . ."

Mr. Harrison glanced at his son, then at Mr. Lee, then at his wife. "Wait, Elizabeth. Billy is younger than Benjy and Carter were when I first sent them on errands, but he's a responsible boy. Perhaps with a groom — and Mr. Lee. . ."

"I'd be happy to look after him and start him on his way back," Mr. Lee said.

Billy's eyes were shining.

The next morning he mounted Brownie and rode proudly away with Mr. Lee.

At noon they stopped at an inn not far from

Williamsburg to rest the horses and eat. "Tonight we'll put up at the Raleigh Tavern," Mr. Lee said.

"I'd like to see the Governor's Palace in Williamsburg, and the place where Father went to college."

Just then they heard the sound of galloping hoofs on the road. They both looked up. Other guests hurried to the windows. Suddenly a dusty figure burst into the room.

"News from the north! General Arnold has deserted to the British!"

Mr. Lee dropped his knife and jumped to his feet. "Arnold! Not Benedict Arnold?"

The messenger nodded. For a moment everyone was shocked into silence. Then the men all began to ask questions. Everyone wanted to know the details.

The messenger talked only as long as it took for a fresh horse to be saddled. As soon as it was brought he mounted and galloped away toward Norfolk.

Mr. Lee came back to the table. "It's hard to believe. Arnold was one of our best and bravest generals—and now he's a traitor. He planned to surrender the fort at West Point without a fight. When the plot was discovered, he left his men and deserted to the British. He betrayed a trust—the most important command we had."

Billy felt uneasy. "Will we lose the war now?"

"No one knows. We still have General Washington and other good men who believe in our cause. Washington is now at West Point. But Arnold's treason is a great loss."

"We still have Colonel Lee, too," Billy said.

Richard Henry Lee smiled. "It's a pity Arnold wasn't as faithful to his ideals as you are, William Henry. But this news changes our plans. The messenger said the Delegates have been called back to Richmond. I will have to put off my business. Berkeley and the other James River plantations must be informed. Your father will want to leave immediately. Will you take the message back to him?"

"What about his papers?"

"The war comes first. Virginia itself may soon be in danger. I'm sure that Ben would agree. You had better return to Berkeley today."

Billy looked so disappointed that Mr. Lee said, "It would be a great service if you would carry word to other plantations on your way. The situation is serious. Everyone should know and be on guard."

Billy's spirits began to rise. "I could do that," he offered.

"I'll write a message you can show to everyone." Mr. Lee called for paper and pens. As soon as he had written a note, Billy and Sam, the groom, mounted.

At Tedington plantation, Billy rode up to the door.

"Good-by, William Henry. I'm sorry our trip proved so short. Tell your father I'll see him in Richmond tomorrow night." Mr. Lee added to Sam, "Take care of the lad."

"Don't you worry, Master Lee. I'm used to following this boy!"

At Tedington plantation, Billy rode up to the door. Mr. Lightfoot came out to meet him. Billy repeated the messenger's words.

"Great heavens, boy, are you joking?"

"Here's the letter Mr. Lee wrote about it."

"This is shocking news! Why, my son fought under Arnold at Saratoga. Arnold guilty of treason! Come in, boy, and rest for awhile."

"Thank you, sir, but my father must have this message tonight. I want to go on."

He touched Brownie's flanks with his heels and they rode off. At Weyanoke, too, people couldn't believe the news.

"How could Arnold have done it!"

"Are you sure this is true, boy?"

"Will we lose any more generals?"

Billy told them all that Mr. Lee had said, and showed them Mr. Lee's letter.

They stopped at other plantations. At last Sam said, "Master Billy, aren't you mighty tired? Don't you want to stop? I'll go on to Berkeley."

"I am tired," Billy said honestly. "But, Sam, soldiers have to march or ride whether they're tired or not."

When they finally turned into the avenue at Berkeley, it was late in the evening. Candlelight shone from the drawing room. Billy heard Smoky bark. Now that she was near her stable Brownie grew livelier. She trotted briskly up to the porch. Billy slid wearily from his saddle just as his father opened the door.

"William Henry Harrison! I thought you were safe in Williamsburg!"

His cry brought his wife to the door. "Billy! What's happened? Where's Mr. Lee? Where have you been?"

For the last time Billy gave his message. His father's face grew grave. "Arnold's gone over to the enemy," he murmured.

"What will happen now, Ben?" asked Mrs. Harrison.

"There may be a plot for other officers to join him. I'll leave early in the morning for Richmond and see what the news is. Billy, you're a good messenger."

"I'm sorry about the papers, Father."

"Richard Lee was right, Billy. This is more important. And you proved yourself worthy of the trust he had in you. You see, Billy, that's the worst thing about Arnold's treason. General Washington — all of us, in fact — trusted him. And he's betrayed us all. But mark my words, the British will never trust him either. Who wants a man who can be bought?"

"Here you stand and talk while this poor child is worn out. Billy, go up to bed at once. I'll bring you some supper."

Halfway up the stairs, Billy turned and spoke to his father. "We don't need Arnold on our side. We'll show him we can win the war without him."

Chapter 5

The New Tutor

Billy walked slowly out of the house, dragging his feet. His thin face was gloomy.

He sighed. At last he wandered down to the stables. Josh and Ezra were cleaning the stalls.

"Hello, Master Billy," they called.

"What's wrong?" Ezra asked. "You sick today?"

"No," Billy said shortly. He seized a pitchfork and helped them spread clean straw for Brownie. Finally he said, "Maybe you'd better saddle Brownie for me. I'll exercise her as long as I can. This will be the last time." He sounded very sorry for himself.

"Huh?" Josh said. "Master Billy, what's the matter?"

"Something terrible — Father is sending a new tutor for Sally and me . . . today."

"Who is he?" Josh asked.

"Some old man from Pennsylvania named Peter

Muehler. He's coming in a boat. He's going to teach us Latin."

"Sure don't sound like much," Josh said.

"Maybe he'll be a nice old man." Ezra thought this didn't sound so bad. Billy didn't have half as much work as he and Josh.

"I'm not going to like him. All tutors are bad," Billy said firmly. "Carter's used to switch for not studying."

"Will you get switched?" Ezra asked.

Billy nodded. His face was long. "Yes — because I'm not going to study."

Just then they heard quick footsteps. Sally ran into the stables. She was wearing a pretty dress. She seemed happy and excited.

"Hurry, Billy! The boat's coming! Mother started down to the dock. I can hardly wait to see Mr. Muehler." She darted out.

"Sally likes the idea," Billy said bitterly. "I wish the boat had sunk."

He walked as slowly as he could to the dock.

A small boat was getting closer, rowed by two men. In the stern sat a dark figure.

"He ought to be in the army," Billy said.

"I wonder if Mr. Muehler uses switches," Sally said.

Both children stared at the stranger. He had dark hair and a pleasant face. He was not very old. But across his knees lay a stick.

"Look, he's brought a switch," Billy whispered. He stuck out his lower lip. "He'd better not touch me!"

The boatman pulled the boat in. Billy grabbed the rope and helped make it fast. The tutor did not stand up till that was done. Then Billy saw why, and felt ashamed. The stick was a cane. Something was the matter with one of the tutor's legs. The boatman helped him step out. He bowed. "Mistress Harrison?"

"Welcome to Berkeley, Mr. Muehler! This is Miss Sarah, and Master William Henry."

Sally made a nice curtsy. Billy bowed, a very small bow. Mr. Muehler smiled. "Mr. Harrison told me of his fine family. It's a pleasure to meet you."

"The children have had a long vacation. They should both be at their studies. But now come and let me show you to your room. You will have time to rest before dinner."

She and Mr. Muehler walked off. The tutor walked with a stiff leg. Sally said happily, "Oh, doesn't he look nice, Billy?"

Billy didn't answer. His mind was busy with a plan.

At eleven o'clock the next morning three tired boys came across the lawn of Berkeley. They had to pass the guesthouse. Sally and the tutor were sitting on the steps.

She spied her brother. "Billy, come here!"

Billy straightened his shoulders and walked over.

He envied Josh and Ezra. They could go on to the slave quarters, and no one would question them.

"You've been fishing, haven't you? Just wait till Mother sees you. She was awfully angry. You'll probably get a switching!"

It was hard to look the tutor in the face. Finally Billy raised his eyes. Mr. Muehler was smiling! "You didn't have much luck, did you?" he said in a friendly way.

"N-n-no, sir." He looked down at his single fish.

"Billy," Sally broke in, "Mr. Muehler got lame in the war. He was wounded at the battle of Stony Point. He told me all about it. He still has a musket ball in his leg!"

"Were you a soldier?" Billy asked in surprise. "With Mad Anthony Wayne?"

"Yes, I was a lieutenant in the Pennsylvania line."

An officer — a wounded soldier — why, their tutor was a hero! Billy felt dazed.

"Mr. Muehler told me all about it," Sally said importantly. "He doesn't believe in having lessons the first day, before we're acquainted."

Billy had never met anyone who had been at Stony Point. There were ever so many things he wanted to know about the battle. "Did you see Colonel Lee there?" he asked.

"Light-Horse Harry? Yes, indeed. He commanded the only cavalry that was with us."

"I'm sorry, sir. But. . . but. . . well, I didn't know you were a *soldier*."

"Billy wants to be a cavalryman," Sally explained. "He won't play anything but war games."

Billy realized what a mistake he had made. "I'm sorry, sir. But. . . but. . . well, I didn't know you were a *soldier*."

Mr. Muehler smiled. "I accept your apology. Army discipline would be more strict, and if I were in the army I'd have to punish you. But I've resigned my commission. I hope you'll think of me as your friend. But I do believe firmly in following the orders of the day. Your father wanted you to have lessons every morning — aren't those your orders of the day?"

"Yes, sir. I'll be here tomorrow. I'll even learn Latin."

"We'll have Latin sometimes, of course, and Greek, and the other things your parents want you to learn. But first we'll have some reading and writing and arithmetic. And something about the battles the colonies are fighting now. . . ."

"That doesn't sound bad," Billy said. "Maybe Sally ought to hear some more about Stony Point tomorrow," he added hopefully.

Mr. Muehler laughed. "That's the battle I know best, Billy. You'll hear plenty about it."

"I'll go give my fish to Mother and get my whipping," Billy said bravely. "Then I'll be ready to report for duty in the morning, sir."

Chapter 6

The Christmas Task

The Harrison family was finishing breakfast a few days before Christmas.

They were a big family now. Mr. Harrison had ridden in from Richmond the night before. Two of Billy's married sisters had come for Christmas.

Billy glanced around the big table at his mother, Sally, Elizabeth, Anna, and Anna's three little girls. He caught his father's eye.

Mr. Harrison smiled. "We men are outnumbered, Billy."

"When are Benny and Carter coming?" Anna asked.

"Benjy wrote me that he couldn't get leave," Mr. Harrison said. "The Southern Army is seeing action now. But things are still quiet in Virginia. The militia will probably let Carter come home the day before Christmas."

"That's the day Lucy is coming," Mrs. Harrison said. "She didn't want to bring the baby earlier. I'll be glad to have my three big girls all home at once."

"I want to see my new nephew," Billy said. "It's about time there was another boy in this family."

"It should be a joyful Christmas," Mr. Harrison said. "And I want it to be one we will all remember happily, in spite of the war. That reminds me, Billy — I have a Christmas task for you."

Billy knew from the way his father smiled that the task would not be disagreeable. "What is it?"

Mr. Harrison whispered, "Come with me and I'll tell you."

Billy followed his father down the hall to his office. There Mr. Harrison kept his desk, his books and the ledgers of the plantation business.

"Sit down," Mr. Harrison invited, "while we transact our business." He motioned to a chair. "I'm going to tell you a story first. Some of it you know, but I want you to hear it all."

Billy sat down and waited. Mr. Harrison paced back and forth between the desk and the bookcase for a few moments.

"Back in 1774," he began, "when you were a year old, the colonies began to have trouble with England. They all sent delegates to a meeting in Philadelphia. I was one of those who went for

Virginia. We talked about our troubles. Finally we sent a list of complaints to the king and told him we thought that the government in England had taken away some of our rights."

He stopped and looked at his son. Billy thought he understood, so he nodded.

"Then we promised to meet again the next year," his father continued. "But by that time there was fighting up in Massachusetts."

"I know," Billy said. "At Lexington and Concord. Mr. Muehler told me all about the battles."

"That's right, son. Since the northern colonies were already fighting, we appointed a general to command their troops. That was my friend George Washington."

Mr. Harrison often talked of him. General Washington had visited at Berkeley, but Billy had been too small to remember him.

"Some of us delegates began talking about becoming independent states, since England was making war on us. We thought we could unite to become a new country and govern ourselves. Here in Virginia we had already tried our own government, with a Bill of Rights to explain what we were doing and what we thought a government should be. I had a hand in writing that bill, son, and I'm very proud of it!

"Well, in 1776 we told the other men that we should declare ourselves independent of England and tell the world why. Richard Henry Lee proposed this, and I backed him up. The men chose a committee to consider the idea and then Tom Jefferson wrote out a report for us."

Now Billy could guess what his father was talking about. "The Declaration of Independence?"

Mr. Harrison beamed. "Yes. I read it to the other members when it was finished. And I was one of the men who signed it. Now, Billy, that Declaration marks the beginning of our country. It tells what we are fighting for. Don't you think you ought to learn some of it by heart?"

"How much of it?" Billy asked in alarm.

"I hope you can memorize the first and last parts of it by Christmas Day and recite them for us. You have no lessons to study this week, and Mr. Muehler will help you with it. Look!"

Mr. Harrison went to the bookcase and pulled out a pamphlet. "It's in here."

Billy got up and looked at the page. It seemed full of very small type and very long words.

"I just want you to learn this first section and the last — not the grievances. You may not know all the words, but I'll explain them as you go along. Take just a sentence or two at a time. It will be a nice surprise for the family on Christmas Day."

"It will be hard," said Billy uneasily.

"Perhaps," said his father, "but I want you to understand how the leading men felt at a very important time in America."

Billy and Mr. Muehler spent hours going over the sentences. It was hard to find a quiet place to practice. The girls were in and out of every room, and his three young nieces wanted him to play.

But on Christmas Day, just before dinner, Mr. Harrison called everyone into the big drawing room. "Billy and I have a surprise for you," he said.

Everyone looked at Billy. He stood up. He was dressed in his best silk shirt and velvet suit. There were lace ruffles at his wrists. His hair was tied back with a black ribbon. He felt stiff and uncomfortable.

"When in the course of human events," he began, "it becomes necessary for one people to. . . to dissolve the political bonds that that have connected them with another . . ."

A week ago he would not have known what all these words meant. But Mr. Muehler had explained them all. He went on, awkwardly but steadily. He stumbled over two words. Once Mr. Muehler had to whisper a word to him. But when he came to the ending he spoke more smoothly.

"And for the support of this Declaration, with a firm reliance on the protection of Divine

Providence, we mutually pledge to each other our lives, our fortunes and our sacred honor!"

He was through, but everyone looked solemn. Nobody said anything. Billy wondered if he should bow, or say "the end"? Then he had a flash of inspiration. He cried out: "Signed by my father!"

Everyone laughed. Carter began to clap his hands and all the others clapped, too. Mrs. Harrison got up and kissed Billy, and his father patted his shoulder. He looked very pleased.

"Now let's have dinner, " said Billy. "I'm starving!"

Chapter 7

Berkeley in Danger

A few days after Billy's performance, a horseman galloped up the drive to Berkeley. He was riding so fast that his coattails streamed out behind him.

Mr. Harrison hurried to the door. Billy ran after him.

The rider reined in sharply at the porch. His horse reared up. "The British!" he called hoarsely.

Mr. Harrison ran down the steps and grabbed the bridle. "What's that?"

"Twenty-seven sail sighted at the mouth of the James. The British are coming!"

Billy felt a tingle of excitement. "Will they sail all the way up the river?"

"There's nothing to stop them from landing anywhere, lad."

Carter Harrison, in his blue militia uniform, came running out and heard the news.

"Got to get on to Richmond." The messenger touched his spurs to his horse and was off again, as suddenly as he had come. The three Harrisons silently watched him out of sight. Carter spoke first.

"This means action for the militia. I'd better report to Williamsburg at once. Will you go up to Richmond, Father?"

Mr. Harrison scowled. "Yes, but I must be sure first that the family is safe. I'll ride downriver with you. Perhaps I can pick up more news."

"Will I get to see a battle?" Billy asked. "Here on the river?" It was hard to imagine warships and blazing cannon on the broad, peaceful James.

"Well, you may see some redcoats at last, son. This may be the action Virginia has feared — an invasion aimed at Richmond. But come, let's tell Mother."

Mrs. Harrison and the girls were all upset by the news. Carter quickly gathered up his gear. Josh brought his horse and Mr. Harrison's to the door. Before Mr. Harrison mounted Billy heard him say softly to his wife, "Tell the girls to pack and be ready to leave in a hurry. You'd better get things ready, too. I don't like the sound of this. I'll be back as soon as I can."

But Mr. Harrison did not come back that night. He did not return until late the next afternoon.

"The British haven't landed," he said as soon as he dismounted.

"Have they gone away?" Billy asked.

"No! The ships are coming up the river. And the militia doesn't have enough cannon to stop them."

Mrs. Harrison and the girls turned pale.

"And in command," Mr. Harrison added, "the British have — Benedict Arnold!"

"Oh, no !" said Mrs. Harrison. "What shall we do?"

Mr. Harrison looked at the circle of anxious faces. "When he must, General Washington retreats to save his army and fight another day. That's what we'll do. I'm sure they're bound for Richmond. They'll plunder whatever they can along the way."

"Let's stay and fight!" Billy said.

Mr. Harrison smiled. "It wouldn't be wise, Billy. I have a better campaign plan. You can be captain. Mr. Muehler will be a colonel. The girls will be lieutenants, Mother will be the quartermaster and I'll be the general. How's that?"

Mr. Harrison sounded cheerful. Even Mrs. Harrison smiled a little.

"Now we'll have a council of war on the evacuation of Fort Berkeley. Lieutenant Anna, you live the farthest west. May we retreat to Springfield and camp with you?"

"Of course, Father. You're all welcome."

"Then we'll start tomorrow, as early as possible. Lieutenant Sally, you help your mother get her silver and china together. Captain Billy, please run and tell Mr. Collins I want to see him immediately."

When Billy came back he found everybody hurrying around, packing clothes and bedding into boxes and trunks.

"Besides this, we can take only jewelry and medicine," Mrs. Harrison was saying. "We'll have to leave the china and silver." She caught sight of Billy. "You may take small things you can carry, Billy."

Billy went up to his room. What would he need at Springfield? His bow and arrows and his kite frame stood in the corner. They were too large. Billy looked at his collection of butterflies and moths. It had taken him a long time to catch them, but they would be hard to carry. He opened the drawer of the highboy where he kept his treasures. He had some pieces of colored glass, three tops, a fife, and many little figures he had carved.

"I'll take my knife," he decided. "And my sling. They can go in my pockets." His eyes went back to his carvings. He was very proud of them, especially two of Brownie. "Maybe I can hide them," he thought.

He put all the figures in a small box with leather hinges. Benjy had made it for him. Then

Billy put all his other treasures carefully away, before his mother came in to tell him to go to bed.

The next thing he knew Peony was shaking him awake. "Master Billy! Come now! Everybody's up. Your breakfast's ready."

He opened his eyes sleepily. Then he remembered. He was Captain Billy now, and they were leaving Berkeley. He jumped out of bed, dressed quickly, and ran downstairs.

"Eat a good breakfast," his mother said. "Then I want you to help me."

Sally was the only one left at the table. "Father says I can ride, too. The carriages will be full of baskets and boxes, and the little children."

After breakfast Billy went to find his mother. She was talking to Abe and some of the other slaves. They had packed the silver and the best china into some boxes. The men carried these out to a corner of the cotton field, where they had dug a big hole. The men quickly lowered the boxes into the hole and threw the earth back over them.

"We won't mark this spot, Billy," Mrs. Harrison said. "But I want you to notice and remember exactly where it is."

"So we'll know where to dig when we come back?"

She nodded. Billy looked around. It would be easy to remember.

As they went back, Billy thought of his own secret. He ran up to get his box of carvings. Everyone was too busy to pay attention to him. Billy brought the box down and then got a shovel. He had already decided on his hiding place, near the biggest elm tree on the front lawn.

He marked off a square of sod first and lifted it carefully. Then he dug a shallow hole and placed his box in it. He covered it and replaced the sod. There was a little heap of dirt left over. He scattered it lightly over the lawn.

At last there was no trace of his digging. Billy hurried back to the house.

The carriages now stood before the porch. The servants were loading them with baskets and boxes, and then Mr. Harrison's saddlebags. Billy knew they were full of papers and letters.

Behind the carriages were three wagons. One was loaded with hay for the horses. Another was filled with hams, potatoes, sugar, flour — all the food the Harrisons could take. The third was for the house slaves to ride in. The field hands would stay at Berkeley. The British were not likely to take them prisoner, and they would drive the horses and cattle into the woods if the British came.

Ezra had saddled Brownie for Billy and was holding the bridle. Billy climbed into the

Billy marked off a square of sod first and lifted it carefully. Then he dug a shallow hole and placed his box in it.

saddle. Brownie seemed frisky and ready to go. He had trouble holding her in while his father mounted and the older girls and their mother got into the carriages.

"All right, Captain and Lieutenant," Mr. Harrison called to Billy and Sally. "Fall in."

Billy spoke to Brownie and trotted down the avenue, followed by his sister and his father. Suddenly he didn't feel excited and happy about going to Springfield. He wished he hadn't heard what his mother said. Then Billy remembered the words of the Declaration of Independence about the king: "He has plundered our seas, burnt our towns and destroyed the lives of our people."

"What are you saying?" Sally asked.

Billy understood better now how those men in Philadelphia had felt when they put their name to the Declaration. He turned to look at Sally and his father.

"We mutually pledge to each other our lives, our fortunes and our sacred honor!"

Chapter 8

Tarleton's Trooper

One May morning in 1781, Billy and Sally sat on the steps of their sister's house in Springfield. They had left Berkeley only a few months before. At last Billy broke the silence. "Everyone's probably planting at home now."

Sally nodded. "I'd like to see Berkeley, and the river," she said sadly. "I wish old General Arnold would go away! I don't care if the redcoats have burned our furniture and stolen all our stock. I'd like to be at home."

"I'm tired of Springfield! Now that Mr. Muehler's gone back to Pennsylvania for the summer there's nothing to do."

They heard the voices of their little nieces inside. "I'm tired of playing with them," Billy said. "They just don't understand about military maneuvers. Let's go for a ride before they come out. I'll saddle up."

When he rode back, leading Sally's horse, Mr. Harrison was on the steps. "Billy, I've just told Sally that you children must keep off the road."

"But, Father, why? Can't we even go riding?"

"You know the British are holding Richmond. I've just learned that there's a troop of British cavalry under Colonel Tarleton making raids in this neighborhood."

"I'm not afraid of any redcoats." Billy was secretly longing to meet some.

"I know you're not afraid. And the soldiers might not harm you or Sally, but they might take your horses. You don't want to lose Brownie, do you?"

"May we ride in the fields?"

Mr. Harrison hesitated. "Yes, if you see no strangers about."

As he rode along with his sister, Billy planned. "Let's go down to the edge of the tobacco field. There are trees all along it and no one could see us. We'll keep a watch on the road. That's what a spy would do."

Sally agreed. Billy peered through the trees down the long straight road. "Look, there's a cloud of dust in the distance!"

Sally glanced in the direction he pointed. "It's just the wind."

"No, Sally, it's getting larger all the time. I think I can see something. . . ."

Now Sally looked excited. "I'm afraid it's men on horseback!"

"I hope it is," Billy said boldly. "I'm right, Sally! They are horsemen. That must be Tarleton's cavalry! Come on!" He wheeled Brownie and rode back to the house as fast as he could go, with Sally right behind. Billy shouted, "The raiders are coming!"

Mr. Harrison ordered everyone inside. The servants ran around bolting the doors and fastening the heavy shutters. The men got their pistols. Billy stationed himself by a window to watch.

Now they could all hear the thunder of hoofs. The first riders swept past the house. Then came the main body of cavalry, riding hard. Some glanced toward the house, but not one stopped. They all galloped on.

Billy realized he had been holding his breath. "Where do you think they're going, Father?"

"Back to Richmond, probably. Thank heaven they didn't stop!"

"May I go out?"

"No!" said Mrs. Harrison.

"There may be stragglers," his father explained. "Troopers who have dropped behind. They are the ones who will cause trouble."

For several hours the Harrisons all stayed in the closed, locked house. They kept a watch at the windows. But no other riders appeared. At last Billy was allowed to go out.

He quickly went to get Brownie. Before he could be told to stay close to the house, he cantered down to the road. There was no one in sight. He rode for a mile without seeing anyone. In the distance smoke hung over the fields, from fires the British must have set.

Suddenly Brownie shied. "Whoa!" Billy pulled her up. "What's the matter, Brownie? What scared you?"

He turned Brownie around and noticed something white beside the road. She didn't want to approach it, but Billy urged her closer. Then Billy saw it was a man, lying face down. He wore no coat or hat. A saber was fastened to his belt.

Billy stared in surprise for a moment. The man moved his head and tried to raise himself. He groaned and fell back.

Billy dismounted quickly. He dropped Brownie's reins and went over to the man. "Hello! Are you hurt?"

The man nodded weakly. Billy could see a dark stain on his shoulder. He knelt beside him. "Can you roll over if I help?" He tugged and pushed. The soldier slowly rolled over on his back. On his right shoulder there was a crimson patch.

"Fell behind. . . . My horse cast a shoe. Somebody took a shot at me . . . fell off . . . walked till I dropped . . ."

While he talked Billy noticed the man's belt buckle. It bore a coat of arms that he knew was not American. Billy realized he must be one of Tarleton's troopers — an enemy!

He couldn't leave the man. That wouldn't be right. Billy remembered a story Mr. Muehler had once read to him, about a soldier who had helped the wounded enemy he had captured.

He looked around quickly. The man had no weapon but the saber. "Why, I've captured a British soldier!" Billy thought.

He knew the man couldn't just stay here, wounded, in the sun. If Billy was going to be a doctor, here was a chance to practice.

"Can you get your shirt off? I can fix up your wound. . . maybe."

The soldier opened his eyes. "Tear it off — but easy, lad."

Billy ripped the shirt off. He did not touch the cloth over the wound until he had soaked it with water. Then he pulled it away gently, and carefully washed off the blood. It came from a ragged gash that was still bleeding.

Billy made a pad from part of the shirt and bound it over the wound. It wasn't a good bandage. It was hard to make it tight enough.

"You're a smart lad," the soldier said at last.

"Can you get your shirt off? I can fix up your wound . . . maybe."

"Could you get up on my horse if I helped you?"

"Give me another drink, and I'll try." He did not ask where they were going.

Billy caught up Brownie's reins and brought her closer. Then he helped the man to his knees. The soldier took hold of one stirrup and pulled himself up painfully. He swayed even though he clung to the saddle.

With effort Billy lifted one of the man's feet into the stirrup. Then he ran around and stepped up into the other stirrup himself. "Now I'll grab your belt and pull. See if you can swing over."

He pulled hard. The man rolled awkwardly onto the horse. He groaned terribly with every breath. Billy slid down. The man slumped over onto Brownie's neck. Billy saw that the soldier's feet were secure in the stirrups. Then he took the reins and led Brownie back home.

The Harrisons saw Billy coming. They met him at the door and helped lift the soldier down. Two servants carried him upstairs at once. Mrs. Harrison took off the bandage. "The bullet went right through his shoulder," she said. "He's fainted from loss of blood."

While she put on a clean bandage Billy went outside with his father. "He's a British soldier."

"Yes, Billy, no doubt of it."

"What shall we do with him?"

"I'll send word to the militia. They'll take him away as a prisoner of war."

"Maybe I shouldn't have helped him."

His father turned to him. "No, Billy, you did the right thing. A physician helps people who are suffering, regardless of who they are. I'm proud of you, son. You behaved like a Harrison."

Billy smiled. "I captured an enemy, too."

His father laughed. "That also was like the Harrisons."

Two days later Mr. Harrison called Billy to the door. There stood a Virginia soldier. To his surprise, the soldier saluted him. "I've come for the English prisoner you captured."

"Yes, sir," Billy said. "He's hurt, you know. Will you — "

"We'll take care of him. I've brought a wagon." They helped the Englishman out to the wagon. He thanked the Harrisons for their kindness and then looked at Billy. "Farewell, lad. I'm much obliged to you. It's better for me to be a prisoner than to have died by the roadside. I'd like you to have something in return."

The Virginia soldier stepped forward, holding the Englishman's saber. He presented it to Billy, hilt first.

"Why, thank you!" Billy took the saber carefully. "Good-by, and. . . and good luck!"

Chapter 9

Billy Meets His Hero

Billy wandered into the innyard of the Swan Tavern in Richmond. He waved to the Harrison slaves.

They were camping around the three wagons. He went on to the stables. Their horses were all unharnessed, and had plenty of hay and oats. Billy moved on to Brownie's stall — and stopped suddenly. A strange, blond boy about Billy's own age was patting Brownie's neck.

"Hello," Billy said.

The boy whirled around. "Oh, hello." He stared at Billy. "This is your horse, isn't it?"

"Yes. Her name is Brownie."

"Mighty nice animal."

Billy nodded. He wondered what this strange boy wanted.

"I saw you ride in, and I came around to see

your horse." The boy gave her a final pat and came out. "I used to have one just that same size and color." He bit his lower lip.

"What happened to her?"

"The British took her when they went through here."

Billy understood. "The thieves! I know how I'd feel if I lost Brownie. If we could stay here tomorrow I'd let you ride her."

The boy brightened. "Thanks all the same. My name's Tom Randolph. What's yours?"

Billy told him. "We're on our way home," he added. "We've been away almost a year."

"Why?"

"We had to stay in Springfield with my sister until Lord Cornwallis surrendered at Yorktown. Berkeley — that's where we live — is on the James, and there were redcoats all around. It was lucky for us General Washington brought his army down and made the British surrender."

"Want to walk around the town? I can show you everything."

"Yes! My father's at the House of Delegates, and I didn't want to go shopping with my mother and sister."

When Billy came back his whole family was at the inn. There was a strange expression on Mr. Harrison's face. He looked serious, but he smiled often. He rubbed his hands and stroked his face.

He didn't seem to hear a word Billy said about Tom Randolph.

"What's the matter, Father?" Billy asked at last.

"I hardly know how to tell you. I'm not sure we can return to Berkeley. I . . . ."

"Oh, Ben, not another delay!"

"Governor Nelson resigned today. He was at the Yorktown siege, you know, and now he is ill."

"But what. . . ."

"The General Assembly elected me governor to fill out his term!"

His family was astonished. Then Mrs. Harrison began to cry. "I'm so happy," she explained. "You deserve the honor."

"Governor Harrison," said Billy proudly. "My father is Governor Benjamin Harrison of Virginia. Won't Tom Randolph be surprised!"

The next day the Harrisons moved into the Governor's mansion in Richmond, and their lives changed. Mr. Muehler did not come back. Billy and Sally went to schools in town. Every day seemed like a holiday to Billy. It was fun to have lessons with Tom and other boys.

But at night Billy wished he were at Berkeley. Important visitors came to the Governor's mansion, and every night Billy had to dress up. At dinner he had to watch his table manners. He couldn't interrupt the grownups. If he whispered to Sally, his mother frowned at them. And Billy always had to keep his hands and neck clean and his hair combed.

One afternoon, as she often did, Mrs. Harrison called Billy in. "Richard Henry Lee is coming to dinner and to stay the night. He is bringing a friend with him. I want you to look your best, Billy."

Cleaning up again! Billy stamped up the stairs, and slammed the door. The clothes he had been playing in looked all right. "I won't change. I'll just wash my hands," he decided.

Later his mother called, "Billy! Will you come down now?"

Billy went downstairs.

"William Henry," said Mr. Lee, "I want you to meet my cousin, Light-Horse Harry Lee!"

Billy gasped. He shook hands with the smiling, sandy-haired officer. But he couldn't say a word. General Lee looked so spick and span.

"How do you do, William Henry? Your father tells me you're quite a horseman."

Billy could only nod.

"I would be honored to have you ride with me in the morning," Lee said.

At this, Billy forgot his rumpled clothes and untidy hair. He turned to his father. "Oh, may I — *please?*"

The Governor laughed. "I think you might be excused from school. On the condition that you don't embarrass General Lee with your appearance."

Billy blushed.

The next morning he was up early. He groomed Brownie and saddled her before General Lee had eaten breakfast. Then Billy dashed upstairs. He polished his boots, scrubbed his face and neck and ears and hands, put on a clean shirt, combed his hair, and even cleaned his fingernails again. He brushed his three-cornered hat, put it on, and came down just as the stableboy brought the two horses to the door.

As they rode through town, Billy had never felt so proud. He was riding with Virginia's most famous cavalryman! He wished Tom could see him.

"I have to deliver some papers to an old officer of mine who lives several miles out of town."

The errand did not take long. Billy held the reins of both horses while he waited. When Lee came out he said, "I believe I could ride your horse, Billy. Would you like to ride mine?"

Billy's eyes widened. "Oh, yes, sir!"

He helped General Lee shorten the stirrups. Then he mounted. He was astride Traveller, a real war horse!

"He has a hard mouth," the General cautioned. "And he likes his own way." Billy could feel the

As they rode through town, Billy had never felt so proud.
He was riding with Virginia's most famous calvaryman!

larger, spirited horse grow tense under him. He took a firm grip on the reins. Traveller pranced around while Lee was mounting Brownie. Then they set out at a canter. Billy couldn't help smiling. This was real riding!

They saw a hunter crossing a field toward the road, but they paid no attention to him. Suddenly his gun cracked, and a rabbit leaped high in the air and dashed across the road in front of the horses. Traveller shied in surprise. Billy dropped the reins and grabbed the pommel of the saddle. Then Traveller bolted off the road, straight across the field.

Billy heard General Lee shout, "Whoa, Traveller!" But Billy had no time to think of anything but holding on. He clamped his knees tight to Traveller's sides and leaned over his neck. He grabbed his flying mane and then reached down for the reins. Finally he seized them and slowly pulled up the slack through his fingers. "Whoa, Traveller, whoa!" he repeated.

He wasn't scared, but he wished Traveller weren't going quite so fast. He might step in a hole. Billy pulled on the reins, but Traveller galloped on.

A low fence loomed up. Billy thought he heard General Lee shout, "He'll make it!"

He clutched Traveller's mane again, and gave the horse his head. Then they were sailing up. . .

up — and over! Billy pulled back the reins with all his strength and Traveller stopped.

General Lee came up and seized the bridle. "This old war horse thinks gunfire is the signal for a charge. I knew you wouldn't get hurt if you could stick on. That was good riding, Billy. Any time you want to join my troop I'll take you!"

Chapter 10

The Muster Day Match

Two years later, Billy's father was re-elected governor. Everyone at the Capitol now knew the Harrison boys. Carter was his father's secretary. Billy, who was going on eleven, often ran errands for his brother. If Carter finished work early, he would take Billy and Tom Randolph to the edge of town. He was teaching them to shoot his Pennsylvania long rifle. Billy already knew how to clean and oil it.

"We'll try a longer shot," said Carter one day. He pulled some small white cards from his pocket. "I'll fasten these on the dead tree."

"Do you want to load first, Tom?"

"No—you try."

Billy took a rolled paper of powder from a leather pouch at his side. He tore open one end, and carefully loaded the rifle with powder, ball, and priming.

Then Billy slowly pulled back the hammer that set the trigger, and lifted the butt.

"Hold it tight against your shoulder and it won't kick," Carter advised.

Billy shut his left eye and sighted down the barrel. The white cards on the tree seemed far away. It was hard to aim the muzzle of the rifle. It wavered with his heartbeat.

"You're trying too hard." Carter smiled. "Relax—raise your head and look at me. There. Now aim as quickly as you can and fire."

Billy bent his head over the stock again, raised the end of the barrel and pulled the trigger. There was a sharp crack, and his right shoulder jerked.

Carter ran forward. "You hit it! Just on the corner."

"Good shooting!" Tom exclaimed.

Billy proudly loaded the rifle again. This time he felt confident. But a card fluttered to the ground untouched. Carter found the bullet hole in the bark.

"I guess that first shot was luck."

"Well, you can't hit the mark every time. Try it once more. Then let Tom shoot."

This time Billy hit one of the white cards near the center. He felt better.

Tom took the rifle.

"Try for the top card," Carter encouraged him. "Make believe it's a rabbit."

They were all quiet while Tom aimed. The rifle cracked, and the bullet smacked into the tree. He missed the next time, too, but his third shot pierced the card. "I'm glad that rabbit waited around for me!"

For the next half hour the boys took turns firing.

"You're both getting pretty good," Carter admitted, "but that's all for now."

"Oh, no!" Billy protested. "It's early yet."

"I know, but I have to meet Father. You take the rifle home and clean it well. Remember, I have to carry it on Muster Day." With that he left them.

"May I carry it back, Billy?"

"Yes. I'll take the powder horn and pouch."

"There'll be shooting matches on Muster Day."

"Let's go together, Tom, shall we?"

Tom nodded. "We'll have fun!"

Muster Day, the day for the annual parade and inspection of the militia, dawned clear. A cannon boomed once to open the program. Billy gulped his breakfast and counted his money at the same time.

"Now, Billy, " cautioned his mother, "do be careful."

"All right, Mother. Excuse me." He left the table and ran to meet his friend. "Let's get down to the square before we miss something!"

Wagons filled the streets, and carriages were

arriving. There was color everywhere—the uniforms of militia and a few regular army officers, bright coats of state officials and townspeople. Flags hung from windows and on poles. Banners waved above the tents of traveling shows.

"Look here, Tom!" A man in shirtsleeves was dancing on a rope strung between two trees.

Tom pulled Billy's sleeve. "There's the puppet show yonder."

The boys went in to watch the puppets jerk through their play. It was about an American soldier who had fought King George to win a home for his wife.

They walked farther along the carnival street.

"Ginger cakes! Hot ginger cakes!"

"That's what I want!" Billy cried. "Here, sir! Two cakes, please."

"Yes, sir, my young masters. They make you grow, they make you glow. Two pennies. Thank you, lad."

Billy bit a large corner off the warm, spicy cake. He grinned at Tom, who was chewing happily. "I saw a magician's tent," Tom mumbled. "Let's find it."

When they came out of the magic show, the street was thronged with soldiers. The parade was over.

"We'd better get down to the barbecue pit," said Billy wisely. Across from the Swan Tavern an ox

Wagons filled the streets, and carriages were arriving.
Flags hung from windows and on poles.

was being roasted to feed the militia and visitors.

The boys watched a dozen men set up tables and
slice meat. The smell of roasting meat was delicious.
Just outside the tavern, barrels of cider and ale and
water were set out.

The boys were some of the first to get bread and meat and mugs of cider. They sat down in a shady spot near the tavern.

"Billy!" Carter hurried up in his militia uniform. "There you are! The militia's finished marching. Will you take my rifle home? I just saw—I mean, I'm looking for somebody and—Will you, Billy?"

Billy didn't want to go home yet. Nor did he want to lug the long rifle around. But after all, his brother was teaching him how to shoot. "Well, all right—I'll take it."

"Thanks!" Carter leaned the rifle against a tree, dropped his powder horn and pouch, and hurried off.

"I bet he saw a girl," Tom remarked in disgust.

The boys finished eating and licked their fingers. There was a crowd by the tavern now.

"Right smart-looking rifle ye got there."

Billy looked up. A long-haired boy in buckskins was standing beside the rifle.

"Yes." Billy got to his feet.

"Be it yourn?"

"It's my brother's." Billy wondered about the strange boy's speech, and noticed he eyed the rifle with admiration.

"Mind if I heft it?"

Billy handed the rifle to him. The boy held it expertly. He sighted down the barrel, examined the lock and stock carefully. Then he gave it back. "Like the one my pappy shoots in Kentucky. Purty nice. . . . Kin you shoot it?"

"I'll say he can," Tom spoke up. "Best shot in Richmond."

Billy wished Tom hadn't said that. He glared at him.

"I kin kill a squirrel at a hundred paces," the boy said quietly.

"I don't believe it!" Tom said.

The boy's face got red. Then he shrugged. "Maybe I could shoot them words out o' yer mouth."

Billy heard laughter. Several men had been listening. One stepped up. "The shooting matches will start soon. I think we ought to begin with these dead-eyed squirrel hunters, don't you, men?"

The others laughed and agreed. "Bring 'em along! They can match while the crowd's gathering."

"Now see what you've done!" Billy whispered to Tom.

"You can beat him," Tom declared. "I bet he's never seen a rifle as good as Carter's. Come on." So Billy carried the rifle to the open ground behind the tavern, where the shooting matches were held. The man who had spoken to him set up shingle marks. Then he clapped his hands for silence.

"Folks, we're starting early with a special match between two boys. One is said to be the best shot in Richmond." The crowd laughed. "The other is the best shot in Kentucky." The laughter spread. "We'll allow them seven shots apiece at forty paces, holding the rifle free. Let's all hope they hit something!"

The crowd laughed again.

"Just a minute, folks, and I'll announce their names." He turned to the boys and bent his head. When he straightened up, he held up his hand. "Folks, you're going to be surprised! The local lad

79

is Billy Harrison, son of our Governor!" There was a moment's silence, and then Billy heard the crowd cheer. The strange boy looked at him with his mouth open.

"The visiting boy, ladies and gentlemen, is Jesse Boone, son of that great patriot, frontiersman and scout of all our Western country, Daniel Boone!"

The crowd cheered again. It was Billy's turn to stare at the buckskin boy with surprise. Everyone had heard of Daniel Boone. He had saved the Kentucky settlements during the war. Billy glanced at Tom. His friend looked a little sick now.

"Hello, Jesse." Billy held out his hand. "I've heard about your father."

Jesse shook hands and smiled. "I've heard about yourn, too."

"Are you ready?" the man asked. "Who'll shoot first?"

"Jesse ought to have a couple of practice shots," Billy said. "He's never used this rifle before."

Jesse Boone knew how to load and prime the long rifle. He planted his feet firmly, lifted the gun and fired quickly. He missed. The second time he clipped the mark, and everyone clapped.

"Now we begin!" the man shouted.

"You first," Jesse said. He handed the rifle back to Billy.

Billy loaded, aimed easily and fired.

Billy loaded, aimed easily and fired. The shingle mark broke. He'd made one hit! The crowd bothered him, though. He fired again and hit. His confidence grew. But his third shot went wild. The fourth and fifth were good. Then the gun began to feel heavy and his last two shots went astray. Well, four out of seven was better than he'd thought he could do. The crowd cheered him.

"Here you are," he said to Jesse.

The boy knew what he was doing, Billy saw. He paid no attention to the crowd. He hit the mark three times running, then missed. He hit it again and missed. On the last shot he hit. The crowd cheered him loudly.

"Five out of seven!" the man called. "The winner! You're a chip off the old block, Jesse. Your father must hear of this. A fine match, boys. You're real marksmen."

"Much obliged for usin' your rifle," Jesse said. "I wish you could come out to Kentucky. I'd like to take you hunting."

Billy glowed. This meant more than winning the match. "I'd like to go west, too." They shook hands again. Billy had lost a match, but he had won a friend.

Chapter 11

William Henry Tries to Be a Doctor

Governor Harrison did not run for office again. "I must look after my plantation, or I will have no money at all, and no land to leave to my sons." The family returned to Berkeley.

Billy was glad to be home. But he was older now, and ready to take on more responsibilities, even if he did not know what he would do in the future. His father put him in charge of some land, and he raised a crop of tobacco on it.

All went well, until he and his father transported both of their crops to the Petersburg market in the Harrison barge.

On the way up river, Mr. Harrison had the tiller. Billy sat on one side where he could look ahead. He began to feel drowsy in the warm sunlight. He shut his eyes for a moment. When he opened them he

"Father!" Billy yelled. He lunged against Mr. Harrison and pushed the tiller hard over.

saw a loaded ferry crossing the river. As he watched sleepily it grew larger, came closer. Suddenly Billy was wide-awake. They were going to collide with that boat!

"Father!" he yelled. He lunged against Mr.

Harrison and pushed the tiller hard over.

The barge rocked dangerously. The men all shouted. They began to back water with their oars, and the boat swung around. The ferry slipped past with only a few inches to spare.

"Whew!" Mr. Harrison wiped perspiration from his white face. "I'm afraid I dozed off. If we'd hit that boat we would have lost our tobacco. Billy, you saved our cargo!"

The rest of the trip to Petersburg passed without incident. At the market, they sold their cargo for a good price. But on their return trip, Billy began to feel dizzy. Was it the sun or the movement of the boat? He looked toward the shore. The trees were all a blur. He slumped down.

"What's the matter, Billy?"

"I don't know," he said in a small voice. "I feel sick."

Mr. Harrison felt Billy's forehead and frowned. Billy felt hotter and dizzier. He dozed a little. He barely remembered when his father carried him up from the dock and into the house.

When he awoke in the morning, a strange man was sitting beside his bed. No, it was not a stranger; it was Dr. Andrew Leiper, from Richmond, twenty miles away. He had often attended members of the Harrison family.

"What—what's the matter with me?"

Dr. Leiper smiled. "I think you got some bad drinking water in Petersburg. Your mother feared it was typhoid fever, but it isn't."

"Do I have to take medicine?"

"I've made you some pills of Peruvian bark. Do you know what that is?"

Billy shook his head.

"There's quinine in it and that's good for fevers. The bark comes from trees in Peru. The Indians used it, and when missionaries went down there years ago they learned about it."

Billy swallowed one of the big pills without objecting. He took a drink of water. "Do you have to open a vein and take out some of my blood?"

"No, I won't bleed you today. Dr. Rush thinks it helps when the patient has a high fever. But some doctors now think it isn't good for sick people, and I'm inclined to agree. You should be all right now in two or three days."

"William Henry, you must think of your future." Three years later, Billy was fifteen. He had grown into a tall, thin boy. Now only his mother and sisters called him Billy. When he came home from school at Southampton even his father began to call him by his full name.

"I'm worried about your education," Mr. Harrison went on. "You've learned a good deal from tutors. You did well at the academies at Hampden-Sydney and Southampton. But you don't want to go on to college. What do you want to do?"

William Henry hesitated. He remembered the help he had given the sick and wounded. And he remembered Dr. Leiper's skillful care when he was ill. "I know you and Mother want me to be a doctor, but I'm not sure. It does make me feel good to help people who are sick or hurt, but somehow that doesn't seem so *exciting* as the things other people in our family have done. All the other Harrisons really helped make history."

"It's true they all served their country," his father said. "But it is also important to serve the people of our country. That's one of the ideals of our new United States."

"I wish I could try being a doctor for a while, and make sure."

"Many physicians have helpers or apprentices."

"Couldn't I be an apprentice?" William Henry asked eagerly. "Then if I decide that's what I want to do I could go to school and study medicine. If I change my mind I'll find some other work."

"It may be hard work. You won't be your own master. You will have to run errands," Mr. Harrison warned.

"I won't mind. Wouldn't I be learning about medicine?"

"Yes, if we can find a good physician who will take you."

"Let's ask Dr. Leiper in Richmond first," William Henry suggested.

Two months later William Henry stood by a table

in Dr. Leiper's house, pounding sulphur in a mortar with a pestle. He stared out the window at a sunny fall day. He wished he could be outside, riding. But already he had learned that a doctor and a doctor's apprentice had little time of their own.

This afternoon William Henry had to make two poultices and take them to patients. He had to deliver pills to three others. Then he was to meet Dr. Leiper and go with him to bleed a man who had a high fever. Dr. Leiper was going to let him make the cut with the spring knife and bleed the patient himself. Then they would go on to change bandages.

Thump, thump, thump! Someone was knocking at the door. A frantic voice called, "Dr. Leiper! Dr. Leiper!"

William Henry sprang to open it. A man stood there panting. He wore a carpenter's apron.

"Where's the doctor? There's been an accident! A scaffold broke—two men hurt badly..."

"Dr. Leiper's out, but I know where to find him. Where are the men?"

"Third square west. One broke his leg."

"We'll hurry."

A broken leg! They would need the long splints. The four thin oak poles wound with strips of canvas stood in one corner. William Henry grabbed them and dashed out.

This afternoon William Henry had to make two poultices and take them to patients.

He ran all the way to the house where the doctor was treating a sick child. Dr. Leiper was just coming down the steps.

They both hurried to the scene of the accident. The carpenters had been working on a new house. A crowd had already gathered around the building.

William Henry and the doctor pushed through.

By the wall lay two men. Both were very pale. One held his shoulder and moaned. The other's face was covered with perspiration, but he was shivering. His leg was bent under him at a queer angle.

Dr. Leiper quickly examined them. "I'll take the shoulder first. It's dislocated, but I can fix it quickly. I need something to sit on — William Henry, get me a sawhorse."

Dr. Leiper helped the injured man sit up. Then he sat on the horse. He grasped the man's bent elbow and wrist with both hands. Then he raised his foot and braced it under the man's arm.

"I have to pull," Dr. Leiper explained, "because the shoulder bone is out of its socket. Steady, man!" He pulled with all his strength.

The man groaned loudly. "Now a quick twist forward — there! Hear it snap? You're as good as new, my man. But that shoulder may be sore for a while. My boy, I'll need your help with this fractured leg. It takes two men to set one. While I cut off his breeches you unwrap the splints and roll up the tapes."

The doctor pulled out his knife. He slit the man's breeches from belt to knee. William Henry could see a strange bulge of flesh just above the man's knee. The ends of the broken bone overlapped.

"A good clean break," said the doctor. He took off the man's shoe and stocking. "We must pull on his leg until the end of one bone meets the other squarely. You have a splint ready to put under the leg, another on top, and one on each side. Then begin a tight spiral bandage."

William Henry quickly laid out the splints. "Ready, sir."

Dr. Leiper was fumbling in his pocket. He brought out his fat leather purse. "Here, my friend, hold this between your teeth and bite on it if you're in pain. This will not take long." He glanced toward the workmen. "Will one of you hold him tightly, to keep him from slipping?"

A carpenter knelt down and put his arms around the injured man. Dr. Leiper sat on the ground, braced his feet, took hold of the man's foot and began to pull.

William Henry had read in Dr. Leiper's books about setting bones. He knew what was happening. The man's leg muscles had contracted after the fracture. They were resisting the pull. He glanced at the man's face. It was ghastly pale, and shining with perspiration. His teeth were clenching the purse.

"There!" Dr. Leiper panted. The bulge of flesh had gone. The bones had come together smoothly. "Look sharp, lad! Don't jar him!"

William Henry placed the splints. Quickly he began wrapping them to the man's leg with the strips of tape. He pulled them as tightly as he could, around and around and around.

At last he was over the knee, and down around the calf. The man could no longer bend his leg. Dr. Leiper let the man's foot down on the ground as William Henry fastened the tape.

"Good work, William Henry," he said approvingly. "A smooth neat wrapping. Now start another, this time up from the foot. Perhaps this man's friends can find a door to use as a stretcher. Help them carry him home. And then you had better see about our pills and poultices."

After a year William Henry no longer ran to fetch Dr. Leiper for each emergency call. He knew what to do for most accidents. He could set bones and bandage wounds, and treat many diseases.

One day he said to Dr. Leiper, "Do you think I should go to a medical school?"

"By all means. I'd be sorry to lose you, William Henry, for you're the best apprentice I've ever had. You seem to have a knack for it. But you need to learn things I haven't the time to teach you — anatomy, the circulation of the blood, surgery. . . . Why don't you go to Philadelphia?"

"My brother Benjy is living there. I could stay with him."

"Benjamin Rush and William Shippen are both lecturing at the university. They're the finest doctors in the country."

William Henry nodded. "That's what my father says."

The doctor looked at him closely. "William Henry, you aren't excited about this, are you? I don't believe you have your heart in medicine."

"I can't decide," the boy said honestly. "I like to be able to help sick people. But I'm not sure I was cut out to be a doctor. Mother and Father are set on it, though, and . . ." He didn't finish.

"Well, my boy, you must make your own career. What would you rather do?"

William Henry smiled. "I don't know that either." How could he tell Dr. Leiper about the five Benjamins? At last he said, "I like to listen to travelers in the taverns talk about the West. Maybe sometime I can go there. Everything here in Virginia seems so old and settled."

"There will be a great need for doctors on the frontier."

"Yes, I had thought of that. Well, I'd better go to the medical college," William Henry said. "Maybe I'll get inspired."

Chapter 12

The Army Calls

Wᴵilliam Henry was still in Philadelphia in August of 1791. He learned that his father's friend, Richard Henry Lee, was in the city. He was now a senator from Virginia. William Henry went to call on him.

"Soon I shall have to call you doctor, I suppose," said Senator Lee. "When you were a boy, I would have sworn that you'd have a military title."

"That's why I came to see you, Sir. I finished the first term in medical school. Since Father died, I'm not sure I want to go back."

"I see. Well, you've given medicine a fair trial. Is there something else you'd rather do?"

"I — Well, Sir, what do you think of the army?"

Senator Lee smiled. "Your father left you no money when he died, but he did leave you a proud heritage of devotion to his country. That is better than any property. I'm sure he would not want you to continue a medical career if you prefer something else. I think he would be pleased that you want to serve your country. Harrisons always have."

William Henry nodded. "Army service means that I would be sent west. It's a new land and I've always wanted to go out there. It's a chance to do something worthy of my ancestors."

Senator Lee put his hand on William Henry's arm. "The West will need its own leaders. If I were your age I'd go with you."

Three months later Ensign William Henry Harrison was on a flatboat floating down the Ohio River. He had been on the move since September, when he was put in command of eighty recruits. They had marched from Philadelphia over the mountains to Fort Pitt. Then they embarked on the Ohio for the headquarters of the Western army.

As they approached Fort Washington, he could see people run in and out of the stockade. Some came down to the water's edge and waved. The pilot signaled to the five other flatboats. They all turned toward the shore. They ran up to the bluff on which the log fort stood. The recruits began to jump off. They were tired of their long voyage.

"Pilot!" somebody called. "Are you going back to Fort Pitt? We want passage."

As they approached Fort Washington, he could see people run in and out of the stockade.

"Yes!" others cried. "Help us get out of here!"

William Henry was puzzled. "What's the trouble?" he shouted.

"Indians! The soldiers are fleeing."

William Henry looked at his recruits. They stood on the slope, quiet but uneasy. They were looking to see how he would take this shocking news. William Henry was alarmed, but he dared not show it. "It looks as though we've arrived at just the right time. Fall in!"

The men climbed up to the level ground and began to line up, four abreast. William Henry took his place at the head. He saw an officer running toward him. "Ensign Harrison?"

William Henry saluted. "At your service, sir."

"Thank heaven you're here! I'm Lieutenant Denny." They shook hands. "Terrible defeat four days ago about a hundred miles north," he added. "General St. Clair lost two thirds of his men! The survivors fled back here in panic and frightened all the settlers. Everything's in disorder."

"The fort looks strong," William Henry said.

"Oh, we're not abandoning the fort. We can hold off the Indians if they come. But we need all the men we can find."

William Henry marched his men up to the fort. They passed settlers' log cabins, now empty. The gates of the tall stockade were open. Wagons and supplies were parked on the parade ground. At each corner stood a square blockhouse two stories high. Inside, the stockade was lined with low, log buildings.

"Take your men over to the barracks," Lieutenant Denny said, "and then I'll show you your quarters."

Soldiers, many of them wounded, stared dully at the new troops. William Henry found a sergeant and asked him about quarters for the men. "Plenty of empty bunks," the sergeant said. "The men who had 'em will never need 'em again."

William Henry made his way back to the officers' barracks. The brown earth of the parade ground had been trampled hard. He thought of the beautiful lawn and the manor house at Berkeley. This was the end of his journey — a distant outpost, full of tired, wounded soldiers, threatened by Indian warriors. He remembered what President Washington had said in August when William Henry was presented to him:

"You don't resemble your father — except, I hope, in spirit."

Then the big, grave man had signed his commission as ensign.

"Our army is small," he had said. "It is all we can afford, and therefore every man in it is important. You will live in danger and work under hardships in the West. But our country is growing. Merit will be rewarded. We need more young men of your promise."

"I'll do my best," William Henry had answered, "to uphold the family name and the army's honor."

Well, Washington and his soldiers and men like his father had won the Revolution and established a new country. It was up to William Henry to see that this country could grow! Maybe the army had lost one battle. It had not yet given up the West.

William Henry found Lieutenant Denny again. "I'll show you where to go," the lieutenant said. "General St. Clair was wounded, but perhaps he can see you tomorrow." He opened a door into a small room with one bunk. "This is as good as we can offer."

William Henry dropped his knapsack. The room was less than half the size of his room at Berkeley. The walls were made of chinked logs and rough boards. There was a tiny window. William Henry felt lonely and a little homesick.

Then he smiled. "Maybe," he said to himself, "when the first Benjamin Harrison sailed into the James River, he thought Jamestown was a small settlement. Perhaps some Indians ran down to the shore to stare at him. Possibly he wondered what he could ever do in such a wild country. But he stayed. And he helped civilize it, too."

William Henry took a deep breath. He turned and hung his cape on a peg.

Chapter 13

Governor and President William Henry Harrison

Almost a hundred Indian canoes were pulled up on the bank of the Wabash River at Vincennes. Four hundred warriors had climbed out and were looking to their chief, Tecumseh, for a signal. The tall Shawnee raised his hand. "Follow me and listen well."

The Indians went up the sloping lawn toward a big brick house. It was a warm August day in 1810. The braves wore only breechcloths and ornaments. They had no weapons. They came in peace to talk with the Governor of Indiana Territory.

On chairs under a giant walnut tree sat Governor William Henry Harrison, his secretary, and other officials. In spite of the warm weather a small fire was burning near them. This was an important meeting. The leading citizens of

Vincennes watched it from the porch of the house and the edge of the lawn.

William Henry Harrison remembered his first encounter with Tecumseh. That had been at the battle of Fallen Timbers, sixteen years ago. William Henry had been aide-de-camp to General Anthony Wayne. They had fought a great battle with the Indians, on a tract of ground covered with the stumps and trunks of trees uprooted by a cyclone. Wayne's army had won the battle and made a peace treaty with the Northwest Indian tribes.

Since then, William Henry had dealt with the Indians in peaceful ways. President John Adams had made him secretary of the Northwest Territory. Then in 1800 the Northwest Territory was divided. The western part was named Indiana Territory. President Adams had appointed Harrison governor of Indiana Territory.

William Henry moved his family to Vincennes, the new capital. He built a fine house, which he called Grouseland. He had lived here for ten years, and had made many treaties with the Indians to open more land for white settlers in Indiana.

Tecumseh came nearer. William Henry rose.

"Welcome to Grouseland and the capital of Indiana Territory." He raised his right hand in salute. "We are honored to see so many of our red brothers."

Tecumseh stopped a few feet away and raised his hand. "We come unarmed. We have always trusted the word of our brother, the Governor. But the chain of friendship between our peoples has grown rusty. I have come to brighten it."

He squatted down with some of his chiefs. He filled a long pipe with tobacco and lighted it at the fire. William Henry was used to this ceremony. He waited until the pipe was passed. He took a few puffs and then handed it to one of the other chiefs.

"Speak, Tecumseh," he said, "and let us wipe away any stains on the stout chain of long friendship."

Tecumseh stood up. He held out a belt of beaded wampum. "The treaties you made last year at Fort Wayne are not good."

There was a murmur among the Territorial officials. Most Indians did not speak so directly.

"The chiefs of the Miamis, the Delawares and the Potawatomis agreed to them," the Governor said. "They have been paid for the land they gave up"

"They had no right to give up that land." Tecumseh interrupted. "My brother the Prophet and I have united the tribes in a great confederation, like the states of your country. While I was away, you made treaties with some local chiefs. You must deal with me and the council of the confederation."

"The chiefs I talked with have hunted on these lands for a hundred years," William Henry insisted. "You are a newcomer to Indiana. They respect you, but they do not regard you as a great chief over themselves."

Tecumseh threw the belt of wampum to the ground. "They will learn! We sell no more land to the whites. They come and settle. They cut trees and drive out the game we live on. They ruin us and rob us!"

"Those are strong words, Tecumseh."

"We are a strong people. We will not let white men come to our land. Thousands of warriors are ready to raise their hatchets when I give the word."

Harrison jumped up. "Are you threatening war against the United States?"

"You will see," he said quietly. He and his men went back to their canoes.

William Henry made a long report to the government in Washington. He agreed with much that Tecumseh had said. But he believed that the Indians could not stand in the way of a growing nation.

The Secretary of War sent a regiment of soldiers to Vincennes. He ordered Governor Harrison to take an expedition up the Wabash River to Tecumseh's village, to show Tecumseh how strong the United States was.

All that summer of 1811 William Henry trained militia from Kentucky and Indiana. In September they started up the Wabash with the regiment of regulars. There were a thousand men in the expedition. Finally on November 6 they came to the edge of Tecumseh's village near the Tippecanoe River. Harrison sent a scout to the village.

"Tecumseh is away," the scout reported. "His brother the Prophet is there. He will talk to you tomorrow."

The soldiers made a camp, but Harrison warned them to sleep in their clothes and keep their muskets close. At four o'clock the next morning he roused his men while it was still dark, expecting an attack at dawn. Suddenly he heard shots at the edge of the camp.

"Bugler!" Harrison called. "Rally the men!" He mounted his horse to direct the fighting.

The Indians had rushed the tents on one side of the camp. Men were fighting hand to hand in the darkness. Harrison brought up reinforcements and shouted encouragement. He ordered the wounded carried to the center of the camp.

A bullet went through his hat and knocked it off. "Watch out!" an officer called. "You're a good target for them!"

But he stayed in the thick of the fight. Another bullet grazed the side of his head. Blood ran down his cheek.

"They're firing on us from behind!" another officer cried.

The Indians had rushed the tents on one side of the camp. Men were fighting hand to hand in the darkness.

"Hold those lines!" Harrison ordered. "We must keep them out of the camp until it's light.

Then we'll charge!"

The men fought on bravely. After another hour the sky grew light. Harrison rode around to the scattered officers. "Fix bayonets and charge when you hear the bugle. We'll drive them off!"

At the bugle call, the soldiers sprang forward. The warriors tried to stand against them, but had to turn and flee. The battle was over.

"How many men have we lost?" Harrison asked.

The surgeon made a count. "At least sixty are dead, sir, and more than a hundred wounded."

William Henry shook his head silently. "I'll help you with the wounded, Doctor."

Almost thirty years passed. Indiana became a state in the Union. Tecumseh's village was a cornfield now. The battleground became a pleasant grove with a small cemetery in it, six miles from a growing town called Lafayette.

Today, May 29, 1840, the road from the town to the battlefield was crowded with thousands of people. Some walked. Others rode horseback or in wagons or carriages.

"This is the biggest political rally ever held in Indiana," said one rider.

"Why not?" another answered. "We've never had such a popular candidate for President. Old Tippecanoe Harrison!"

A stranger spoke up. "I'm from Kentucky and I fought with him here in 1811. That was only the beginning. He fought all through the War of 1812. I marched with him up to Fort Wayne when we drove off the Indians there. Then we held Fort Meigs on the Maumee River against all the attacks the British and Indians could make."

"Listen, I'm from Ohio," another man said. "We were glad when General Harrison came back from the war and settled near Cincinnati. We sent him to Congress, then to the State Senate, and finally to the United States Senate. We had faith in Harrison because he had fought our battles. Everyone turns to him for advice, and he's done a lot of speaking around the country. He should have won the election in 1836. Now he's running against Martin Van Buren again."

"He'll win this time. There's the old battle-ground! Just look at the crowd!"

A large meadow was filled with tents and wagons. Beyond it the ground sloped up to a grove crowded with men and women. Children danced and chased one another in games.

A marshal was trying to line up the parade.

"Seems as though every county in the state has sent a delegation, besides those from other states."

The chairman of the rally nodded. "There must be at least thirty thousand people here."

The marshal sent men to open a path around the edge of the battleground. Then he signaled the first band to lead off. Behind them came a small full-rigged ship, mounted on wheels and drawn by six gray horses. On the mast was a pennant with the names "Harrison and Tyler."

The people began to cheer. "There's the winning team for President and Vice-President!"

Behind was a drill company in uniform. They carried flags and a banner that said:

"We'll stand for the colors,

Red, white and blue,

And vote for the Hero

Of Tippecanoe."

Next came a small log cabin on wheels. From the chimney streamed another banner. This one read "William Henry Harrison, the Washington of the West."

The parade lasted for more than an hour. When the last group passed, everyone pushed closer to the speakers' stand. The chairman of the rally was shouting for order.

"Tippecanoe and Tyler, too!" the crowd yelled back.

"Ladies and gentlemen! I have the honor to introduce a distinguished company of men: twenty-seven veterans of the Battle of Tippecanoe"

He couldn't go on because of the cheering. The enthusiasm lasted all afternoon. It lasted through the picnic lunch, the speeches praising Harrison, the barbecue supper and the fireworks.

The whole country rallied to William Henry Harrison. By their votes they elected him the ninth President, "the first President to come out of the Northwest Territory," as his friends in Indiana said.

Few were left to remember the little James River boy who had wanted to make his ancestors proud of him.

What Happened Next?

- William Henry Harrison became President of the United States on March 4, 1841.

- After only one month as president, he died on April 4, 1841 from a cold that developed into pneumonia.

- He was the first president to die in office.

- His term in office was the shortest of any president.

- He was the first president to have a campaign slogan—"Tippecanoe and Tyler, too!"

Visit the Publisher's website at www.patriapress.com to learn more about William Henry Harrison.

About the Author

Howard H. Peckham was a professor emeritus of history, Director of the Clements Library at the University of Michigan, and Director of the Indiana Historical Bureau. In addition to his many accomplishments in the field of history, he was a founder and early editor of *American Heritage*. He was the author of numerous historical works for adults, and, in addition to *William Henry Harrison, Young Tippecanoe*, wrote *Pontiac, Young Ottawa Leader* and *Nathanael Greene, Independent Boy*.